Produced by The Creative Spark
San Clemente, California

Illustrated by Yakovetic Productions

Printed in the United States of America.

ISBN 1-56326-157-X

Dear Diary

"For me?" the Little Mermaid said gleefully
as Sebastian handed her the brightly wrapped package. It
wasn't even her birthday, but Ariel's friends were giving her a present!
   "It's for being such a good friend," Sandy the fish said.
   "Go ahead," urged Sandy's brother, Flounder. "Open it!"

Ariel carefully untied the green ribbons and opened the box. Inside was a necklace made of sparkling sapphires and shiny orange coral.

"Oh, it's so beautiful!" she exclaimed.

"Do you really like it?" asked Sebastian.

"I love it!" Ariel said, trying it on.

That night, as she did every night, Ariel wrote in her diary.

Dear Diary,

Today my friends gave me the most beautiful necklace I've ever seen! And tomorrow afternoon, Flounder and Sandy and I are going seaberry picking! I'm so lucky to have such wonderful friends!

The Little Mermaid didn't know it, but Ursula the evil sea witch was watching Ariel in her magic pearl.

"What has she got that I haven't got?" Ursula growled. "Sure she's beautiful. And she can sing, too. But she won't be so popular once I get through with her!"

"I've got it!" Ursula cackled wickedly. "I'll write nasty things about Ariel's friends in her diary. Then I'll trick them into reading it. We'll just see how wonderful Ariel's friends *really* are."

The next morning, while Ariel was away feeding the sea horses, Flounder and Sandy arrived to go seaberry picking.

"What are you doing here?" Flounder asked when he saw Ursula in Ariel's grotto.

"Just catching up on a little reading," replied the sea witch, her tentacles swirling around the diary.

"Hey!" cried Sandy. "You put that back! Ariel doesn't want anybody reading that!"

"I can understand why," Ursula said, "considering all the nasty things she wrote about you."

"What nasty things?" asked Sandy.

"See for yourself," the witch replied coolly as she slithered away.

Everyone knows a diary is a very private thing, and shouldn't be read without the owner's permission. Flounder and Sandy definitely knew this, but their curiosity still got the better of them.

"Dear Diary," Flounder read aloud. "*Today my friends gave me the junkiest piece of jewelry I've ever seen.*"

"Hey!" said Sandy. "She told us she thought it was beautiful!"

"And tomorrow," Flounder continued reading, "*those pesky little fish, Flounder and Sandy, want me to pick seaberries with them. How boring!*"

"And look what she wrote about Sebastian!" Sandy gasped.

Just then, Ariel returned from doing her chores. "I'm ready to go seaberry picking!" she said cheerfully.

Flounder quickly placed the diary back on its shelf. "We're not in the mood anymore," he said.

"Besides," added Sandy, "you'd just be *bored* playing with a couple of pesky fish like us, anyway." And with that, the two of them swam off toward the lagoon.

"That's odd," Ariel said to herself. "I wonder what's gotten into them?"

Flounder and Sandy couldn't wait to tell the others what they had read in Ariel's diary. "It says you're an awful singer, Scales, and that Scuttle is a birdbrain!" Flounder informed them.

"That's terrible!" said Sebastian.

"Oh, I don't know," replied Scuttle. "I *am* a pretty brainy bird."

"I mean it's terrible that they've been reading Ariel's diary," scolded Sebastian. "A diary is something very private."

"She also wrote that you're a bossy little crab who thinks he knows everything," Sandy said.

"She what?" the crab exclaimed. Now Sebastian was upset with Ariel, too.

When Ariel came by to see if anyone else wanted to pick seaberries with her, she got a surprise.

"No, thank you," Scales said frostily. "I might start singing, and I wouldn't want the sound of my voice to disturb you."

"And I wouldn't want you to think I was being bossy and telling you which berries to pick," Sebastian said with a frown.

Ursula saw and heard her plan working perfectly. "Soon Ariel will be everyone's least favorite mermaid," she whispered, as a smile slowly crept across her face.

Ariel picked seaberries all by herself, then swam back to her grotto. She didn't understand why all her friends were being so mean to her. That night she wrote:

Dear Diary,

Today was such an awful day! No one would play with me. It seemed as if they were angry with me about something, but I can't figure out what.

As she put her diary away, Ariel noticed something strange. Someone else had been writing on the pages! And they had written things about her friends that were not very nice at all!

"So *that's* why everyone was so angry!" Ariel exclaimed. "They've been reading my diary!"

Now Ariel had a plan, too.

She wrote in her diary, then made sure to leave it out where everyone could see it.

Ariel hid behind some seaweed and watched as Flounder and Sandy found her diary. The two fish couldn't believe what it said this time! "We'd better show this to the others right away!" cried Sandy.

"Dear Diary," Sebastian read aloud to everyone at the lagoon. "I know what's going on now. My friends have been reading you! I can't believe they would do something so terrible!"

"Ha!" said Scales. "That's not half as terrible as those things she wrote about us!"

"Wait! There's more!" Sebastian said. "It hurts a lot to know my friends don't respect my privacy, but what hurts even more is that they could believe I'd write such things about them! It's not even my handwriting!"

"I thought there was something fishy about Ursula being in the grotto!" said Flounder.

"It was just one of Ursula's tricks," Sebastian said sadly, "and we fell for it."

That night, the Little Mermaid's friends surprised her with another present. "We're sorry we read your diary," Sandy said. "We were wrong and we'll never do it again."

"But just in case," Sebastian added, handing her a package with a big bow tied around it, "we want you to have this."

Ariel quickly tore off the wrapping paper and opened the box. She couldn't believe her eyes. Inside was a shiny gold lock and key.

"It's for your diary," Flounder told her shyly. "To keep out nasty sea witches—and curious fish, too."